The Alternative

Shannon Freeman

D0048362

SADDLEBACK
EDUCATIONAL PUBLISHING

The Most Beautiful Bully

Silentious

The Alternative

All About My Selfie

EDUCATIONAL PUBLISHING
www.sdlback.com

Copyright © 2015 by Saddleback Educational Publishing
All rights reserved. No part of this book may be reproduced in any form or by any means, electronic or mechanical, including photocopying, recording, scanning, or by any information storage and retrieval system, without the written permission of the publisher. SADDLEBACK EDUCATIONAL PUBLISHING and any associated logos are trademarks and/or registered trademarks of Saddleback Educational Publishing.

ISBN-13: 978-1-68021-008-8
ISBN-10: 1-68021-008-4
eBook: 978-1-63078-290-0

Printed in Guangzhou, China
NOR/0515/CA21500758

19 18 17 16 15   1 2 3 4 5

Acknowledgements

Thank you to everyone following my stories and buying my books. The fact that you allow me into your home is a wonderful gift.

Thank to the Port Arthur Alternative Campus staff and students. Many people have passed through those halls and made it what it is today. Thank you for your continuous support. You have inspired a story in me.

To name a few who have influenced our students and made an impact in their lives: Mr. Eddie Fowler, Mr. Luther Thompson, Mrs. Sharon Davis, Ms. Velenta Mathews-Hunter, Miss Evette Rodgers, Mrs. Karesse

Mitchell, Mrs. Shannon Woods Richard, Mrs. Myrna Papa, Mr. David Barnes, Mr. Craig McCabe, Ms. Diasheena Gabriel, Coach Trinidad Rivera, Coach Cornelius Harmon, Mr. James Chavis, Mrs. Carol Gauthier, Miss Lola Higgins, Mrs. Cynthia Gunner, Ms. Patrice Sparks, Mrs. Lynda Hall, Mr. Stillman Hebert, Mr. Darrell Jones, and Mrs. Natasha Crockett.

We have had some interesting times together in the trenches.

Dedication

To those who have been in an alternative school, don't let that fact define you. Allow that experience to sharpen you. If you fail in an area, just keep trying. It's all any of us can do.

Chapter 1

Different Paths

Brent Bonham observed his father's meeting. His dad ran a private boot camp called Living Proof. He started it when he retired from the Marines. Today he was addressing the next graduating class.

Brent had heard it all before.

"You can do this."

"You have everything you need."

"I don't expect to see you back here."

"I am here for you."

It was the same story every three months. The boys in the group looked at Brent like he was lucky to have a father who cared. But Brent didn't feel that way. At home, his dad was cold and distant. He did not care. Brent never wanted to be like his dad.

Brent's personality was more like his mom's. She was warm, funny, charming: a down-to-earth Texas-born girl. She worked as an environmental lobbyist. She was opposed to the area's big oil companies. His mother was a person who fought to make sure that big oil did not play dirty with Texsun City.

Mrs. Bonham had been in Washington, D.C., for a couple of months. That left Brent alone with his father. He begged his mom to come home every time they talked. She always promised that it would be soon.

Brent did have a nanny. She lived in the Bonham house. She had been with them for as long as he could remember. His nanny did everything his parents did not. They were always so busy saving the world. They sometimes forgot about their son's needs.

He was a low-maintenance kid. He never got into trouble and always did what he was told. There were times when rebelling sounded appealing. He wanted to be a free spirit. He would even describe himself that way. But breaking the rules came with weighty consequences. Embarrassing his family was definitely not on his agenda.

There was a mixture of students today at Living Proof. Some of them had been through the boot camp before. A few of them even attended Summit Middle School, where Brent was a seventh grader. He recognized a lot of them, even if they were from across town. He saw them on Friender or FlashChat. With social media, the days of anonymity were long over.

Brent used to sit in these meetings and

not know a soul. But he was catching up to the Living Proof students in age. Slowly, he began to recognize more and more faces.

One person in particular was Coby Reynolds. He had been the leader of his crew since kindergarten. They were hard-core. If there was a fight, Coby and his boys were involved. If there was something stolen, they were involved. Brent typically avoided that type of kid. But they didn't want to hang out with him either. They were on different paths.

Brent sometimes wished he could be as feared as the guys his father mentored. But he didn't even know how to begin. His brain didn't function the way theirs did. He was more straight-laced. He watched them, wondering what their lives were like. Did they go home to cruel and overbearing fathers? Were their mothers at home, making treats and cooking meals?

Brent had a few friends at school, like

Holden, Aiden, and Finn. They were all in the same orbit. First go to Summit. Then to the magnet program for high school students. Then to Texas A&M, UT, or some Ivy League school.

It made him yawn. There was nothing more boring than having your life planned by your parents. Neither of his parents had followed *their* parents' advice. Even their marriage was rebellious. It was the first inter-racial marriage for both families. There were a lot of growing pains all around.

His father's family had taken it the hardest. Brent's mother was not born with a silver spoon in her mouth. She was the first African American Bonham. Brent was the second. She had come from an average middle class family, nothing like his father's.

The Bonhams were one of Texsun City's leading families. They began the oil boom, drilling the original wells. Brent's mother was unaware of this when she met his father. She was political and motivated, fighting for reform in the oil industry. His father found her passion very attractive.

One year after meeting, they married at the courthouse. Then came Brent, their beautiful curly-haired, caramel-colored baby. His parents balanced each other. Brent brought the whole family back together. A lot was expected of him. So much that it stressed him out sometimes.

His relationship with his father was never smooth. Now with his mother out of town, the wrinkles in their relationship seemed even more obvious.

Chapter 2

Hanging Loose

When the meeting was over, the graduates were given instructions for their big day. Then they were dismissed. Some of them stopped near Brent on the way out.

"Let's grab some burgers and go to the seawall," Coby told his crew. When he said to do something, it was already done. Brent smiled as he watched Coby's boys fuss over him. He wished he commanded as much power as Coby. But living under his father's rules didn't give him street cred.

The group started out the door. But then Coby turned around. "Hey, Brent! You wanna roll with us tonight?"

Brent was put on the spot. He had never been invited to roll before. His father would never go for that. "For real? Nah, I better not," he told them, looking back over his shoulder for his dad.

"Why not?" Coby asked him. "Your old man wouldn't like that, huh? You hangin' with the kids he's tryin' to save." The other boys started laughing.

"Nah, it's not like that," Brent said uncomfortably. "I mean … I could roll … I guess."

He went back inside to think of an excuse to tell his father. He had to be quick on his toes. "Hey, Dad," he said, interrupting the meeting his dad was having with his second in charge.

Mr. Bonham turned his attention to his son. "What's up, Brent?"

"I need to go by the library on the way home. I'll meet you at the house."

"I can take you, son. We were just wrapping up."

"No, it's fine. I mean … I'm fine. It's right up the street. I'll see you soon."

He left and walked outside to meet the guys. They'd waited for him. He couldn't believe it. They actually wanted to hang out with him. "Let's roll!" he said excitedly. He looked back over his shoulder to make sure his father wasn't coming out.

"Your dad was cool with you hangin' out with us?" Coby asked him.

"Of course. It's not like it's your first day in the program. It's your last day. He knows you're good dudes."

They went over to Jean's, the neighborhood's best burger joint. They could eat oversized burgers, cheese fries, and a glass of lemonade for five dollars. It was Coby's crew's tradition after they left Living Proof. Brent followed along and watched closely at how they interacted.

He had friends at school. But Summit was different. The students were high achievers focused on making straight As. He didn't have to work hard to get into Summit. His last name bought him a spot at the table. Not to mention that he was smart too.

They quickly ate their food. Then Brent followed Coby and his crew to the seawall. Stars blanketed the evening sky. Barges sounded in the distance. Lights twinkled in the water. Brent felt free. The atmosphere was hypnotic.

"Man, it's chilly out here. I can't wait for spring to come," D-Boy announced. "I need some warmth in my life."

"It feels fine to me," Coby bragged. "It's

a great night for a swim." He began to strip down, like he was going to take a dip.

"You've got to be kidding me. I'm not going in there tonight," D-Boy protested, shaking his head.

"You swam these waters before?" Coby asked Brent.

"Me?" Brent asked, surprised. "No ... I mean the sign says no swimming allowed."

"Do you always follow the rules, dude?" Coby laughed.

Brent thought about it. He prided himself on being a free spirit—on being different from his dad—but he did always follow the rules. There was never a time when he didn't. Tonight, he wanted to live on the edge. "Hey, I'm down," he said with a twinkle in his eye. He stripped down to his boxers and white T-shirt.

Brent got to the edge of the rocky bank and jumped in. Coby slipped on the rocks, hurting his toe. "Dude, you go ahead. I'm bleeding. We just swim to the buoy and come back. I can't make it."

"I'm not going without you," Brent said, treading water.

"Man, you're already in. Don't chicken out now," Coby said.

Brent glanced over at the buoy. It wasn't far. He could make it there and back. Be everyone's hero. He looked back at the guys waiting on the seawall. He kicked forward in the water, swimming as fast as he could. It was cold. But his body quickly adjusted to the temperature.

When he finally reached the buoy, he turned around. He proudly pumped his fist in the air. But Coby and his crew were gone. He only saw red flashing lights. Police cars. *Shoot*, he thought, trying to swim parallel to the shore.

There was no way he was going back the

way he'd come. He could hear a barge horn sound a warning. He looked up to see one coming right at him. He had to make a quick decision. He was panicking and being pulled under the water by the barge. When he came to his senses, he decided to swim back to the rocks.

Turning quickly in that direction, he hit something sharp in the water. It ripped through his shin. He was hurt. He couldn't swim fast enough to get out of the way of the oncoming barge. *This was a bad idea,* he thought.

The more he swam, the more he realized he wasn't moving. The barge was pulling him toward it. Time was not on his side. Just when he thought there was no hope, a boat pulled up next to him. It was the Coast Guard. He felt relief. But that was short-lived. He knew by the looks of the Coast Guard team that he was in a world of trouble.

Chapter 3

Texsun City Alternative Center

His father sat stone-faced all the way to school. When they rounded the corner, Brent could see a sign in the distance: Texsun City Alternative Center.

As they walked into the front office, the receptionist greeted Brent's father excitedly. Brent saw his father in his element for a brief second.

His dad was a handsome man who commanded respect. Brent could tell the ladies flirted with him. Brent didn't like it. His dad was a married man.

"Mister Bonham," the receptionist said, standing up to greet him.

"Don't get up, Bell," Brent's dad said with a smile.

She was an attractive woman with long brunette hair. She wore a white button-down shirt, a black pencil skirt, and a red belt. Brent rolled his eyes as she threw herself at his dad.

"What can we help you with today? Are you enrolling another one of your boys from Living Proof?"

"Not exactly, Bell." His demeanor changed. His whole body stiffened. "This isn't *one* of my boys. This is *my* boy, Brent Bonham. Brent, say hello to Ms. Hadley."

"Hi, Ms. Hadley," Brent said, offering his hand.

"Well, isn't he a gentleman? Just like his father," she said, impressed by Brent's manners. "Well, have a seat, Bonham men. I'll get the counselor for you." She smiled at Brent on her way out and gave him a nod.

She was trying to make him feel more comfortable. Nothing was going to work at this point.

They sat there, father and son, not speaking and trying not to make eye contact. After all, hadn't they said it all the night the cops showed up? Brent had appeared dripping wet on the front doorstep.

His father had looked disheveled on the other side of the door. He had been calling all of Brent's friends, hospitals, and the police. He didn't know what to do. That night felt like the worst night of both their lives. Now here they were. The nightmare continued.

Just as Brent thought it couldn't get any worse, Jessa McCain walked into the office in an all-out rant. She was going on and on about taking off her headband. Everyone in the office could hear her.

"Jessa," Ms. Hadley said as she returned. "You need to calm down, honey. What's the problem?"

"Coach Simms sent me up here. He said I can't wear my flowered headband. He let Melissa wear her headband yesterday. He made a big deal out of nothing. I will call my father and shut this whole operation down," she warned.

"Jessa, your father doesn't work here. He works at the refinery, dear." Ms. Hadley spoke in a patient voice, as if she'd told Jessa this before.

Brent was mesmerized. That headband looked like a halo. *How could anyone ask an angel to take off their halo?* She was like a fantasy, a dream. He'd never been this close to Jessa McCain. Summit Middle School's seventh grade It girl. She was beautiful. But she had a mean streak. He'd heard she was at TAC, and now she was right in front of him. *Maybe this isn't going to be so bad after all. She's the most beautiful girl I've ever seen.*

Caught up in all of Jessa's glory, he never noticed her peering in his direction.

"And what are you looking at?" she asked coldly. Her eyes were narrow slits.

"Who? Me?" Brent stumbled over his words.

"Yeah, you! Why are you gawking at me? Ew!"

"Son?" his dad asked.

"Jessa, don't be rude," Ms. Hadley told her. "Now give me the headband and go to class. Or I will call your father."

Jessa untied the headband and put it on the desk. "Just so you know, there better not be a flower crushed on that headband."

"Jessa, I'm going to lose my patience

with you very soon. You need to leave the office." Ms. Hadley picked up the headband using a napkin, as if it had been contaminated by a virus. She dropped it in the box with all the other confiscated items.

Jessa flounced out in a huff.

Ms. Hadley looked at Mr. Bonham and shrugged her shoulders. "Sorry about that. Just another day at TAC," she said.

The counselor came out just in time to save them from another front office run-in, as one of the boys from Living Proof rounded the corner. They went into the counselor's office. He gently closed the door behind the Bonhams.

He greeted Mr. Bonham and then Brent. Then he invited them to have a seat. "Well, Mister Bonham, I know you know the drill. But do you understand why *you* are here, Brent?" he asked, concerned.

"Not really. I mean … I wasn't even at school when I got in trouble."

"Yes, that is true. But whenever the police have to get involved in an incident like yours, then you have to come through the alternative center before going back to your home campus. We don't have many students here. We run a tight ship. So follow the rules. Then you should be fine."

"Oh, he's going to be fine," his father said, looking at Brent. He was daring him to mess up.

The counselor went over the rules and expectations. Then he introduced Brent to his teachers. His father left him there. The alternative campus was the last place Brent thought he would ever be.

He was *so* nervous. His hands were sweating. He didn't know what to expect from the other students. They looked at him as if he were from another planet. Their eyes searched his, as if that would help them determine why he was sent here. He avoided their curious stares and went to class. It was all so new.

He had never been in trouble. But this time, trouble seemed to have found him.

Chapter 4

Home, Not So Sweet, Home

The dinner table was quieter than usual. The only thing that could be heard was the fork as it hit the plate. Usually his father asked him about his day, his homework, or the upcoming activities he was looking forward to. Today, he sat stoically cutting his steak, chewing, and swallowing. His eyes never looked at his son. They avoided each other's gaze.

Brent secretly wished his mother would walk through the door right then. Everything would change. Her presence brought peace, laughter, and lots of hugs and kisses. It had been a rough day. Today, he wanted someone to talk to. But he knew his father was withdrawing from him. He was still angry that his son was at the alternative center. He was probably embarrassed as well.

Brent tried to say something to his father. It was tough. The words didn't come out. He cleared his throat in a vain effort to spark small talk with him. "Dad, I was thinking …"

His father quickly stood up from the table and retreated to the kitchen. Brent sat staring at his plate. He tried to reach out to his dad. He tried to smooth things over. His dad wasn't having it.

Brent slowly picked up the dinner dishes and brought them to the kitchen. He looked around and felt the emptiness of their home.

A tear slid down his face as he wished for his mother's return. When he was done cleaning the kitchen, he went to his room to video chat with her. Her phone rang two times, then his mother's beautiful brown face appeared before him.

"Hey, baby," she said with a big smile on her face.

"Hey, Mom," he said, smiling.

"How are you today? You don't look so well," she said, sensing his turmoil.

"You know … I'm making it."

"Well, son, it's hard to lie in the bed you make sometimes."

"I know." He looked away. He knew she was disappointed in him. It wasn't a good feeling.

"Soon this will all be a memory. Mama can't wait to get home to you. How are you and your father getting along?"

"We're not. You know Dad. He won't

even look at me. I tried talking to him at dinner. He just left the table."

"You know your father has his own ways of dealing with things. He'll get over it. One thing is for sure, he loves his son. You two will get past this."

"I don't know about that." He tried to fight back the tears. He didn't know if his father would ever forgive him.

"Hey, trust me. It will be fine."

"I love you, Mom. When are you coming home?" he whined. It was like he was five years old again.

"Soon, baby. This is taking a little longer than I anticipated. Don't worry, though. If I can't come home, then you are going to have to come to D.C. to see me. I miss my son," she said sincerely.

"Whoa, Mom. I'd love that! I want to come to D.C."

"Me too. Now let me get back to work. I

have to go over some notes. Call me tomorrow night, okay?"

"You know I will," he promised.

He hung up, feeling somewhat better. She had that effect on him. She was everything a mother should be. He just wished she were home.

That night he tossed and turned in his bed. He couldn't sleep. Just thinking of his dad being mad at him was keeping him awake. He hated going to bed upset. He had to get it off his chest. He walked downstairs to his parents' master suite and knocked on the open door.

"What?" his dad yelled, making him immediately regret taking the walk downstairs.

"Dad, can I have a minute?" He took a deep breath, waiting for his father to snap at him again.

He paused as his father placed his iPad next to him on the bed, his blue eyes peering at his only child as if he had nothing to say to him.

"What now?"

"Look, I know I messed up. I know you're mad at me. But I promise that I will make this up to you. I'll never get in trouble again. I just made a mistake."

His father softened. He knew his son was right. It was one mistake. But he couldn't be soft on him, or he would make another one. Brent couldn't afford to make another mistake. His father knew it could become a pattern if they didn't nip it in the bud.

"Look, son, I don't want you to make this a habit. You know how much I put into those kids at Living Proof. But if you turn into one of them, then none of this is worth it."

He could tell his dad was concerned about him. For the first time it sounded like he wasn't only concerned with his own reputation.

"Dad, I won't let you down. I promise."

"Okay, Brent. Let's get through these thirty days and then put it behind us. Just make sure you stay out of trouble while you're at TAC. The last thing I want is to go there again. Deal?"

"Deal!" Brent said excitedly, hoping that he could make his father proud.

Chapter 5

The Law of the Land

Another day at TAC. Brent was already bored with the atmosphere. He had the same classes with the same people, day after day. He couldn't talk to anyone. And kids got in trouble for every little thing.

The teachers expected the students to jump right into a lesson, even though they'd just arrived at the school. It took a minute for him to even understand where they were in the material. He'd been suspended for a couple of days, so assuming he would pick up where he left off at Summit was insane.

English class was the worst. They were at the end of a novel. The final test was on Friday. When he asked the teacher if he would be required to take the test, she laughed.

"Check out a book and get to reading," was her only advice. By the end of the day, he was loaded down with homework. He had more work to do at TAC than he had at his regular school. He knew if he wanted to get back in his father's good graces, he'd better get it done.

He was drained. He had been up till midnight, getting caught up. But he'd managed to get it done. Now he could move smoothly through his schedule. He was on autopilot. This was going to be a long month.

"Psst." A student was trying to get his attention during math. Brent didn't want to turn around. But he knew he couldn't ignore the kid forever. "Hey, Bonham," the student whispered. "Do you have an extra pencil?"

"Nah, I just brought one with—"

"Mister Bonham? Are you talking?" Mr. Chavez was working out an equation at the board. He turned around quickly.

"No, I was just telling him—"

"You have after school detention tomorrow. There's no talking unless you are called on. Did I call on you?"

"No, sir." Brent looked at the other student, as if he would help him out. But he had no response. The more Brent tried to explain, the more Mr. Chavez dug in his heels. Brent gave up. *How am I supposed to explain to my dad that I have detention on my third day of school?*

That night he came up with a foolproof

plan. He would stay after school and ride the city bus home. That way his father never had to know he had detention.

He showed up at Mr. Chavez's room after school the next day. There were already two other students there. They were writing out the detention agreement. It was a one-page letter. They had to copy the entire thing and sign it. Brent was already annoyed. There had to be something better that he could be doing with his time.

"I will not sleep in class. I will be respectful. I will be on time." The list went on and on. It seemed as though the clock wasn't moving. Every time he looked at it, only one minute had passed. It was the longest thirty minutes of his life.

After the students completed detention, they stood outside to wait for their rides.

"Hey, why are you at TAC?" a Hispanic

student asked curiously. "You don't seem like TAC material."

"I swam the seawall."

"Oh, you're *that* kid? Yo, I watched it go down on FlashChat. I'm Gustavo," he told Brent, stepping in to give him a handshake.

"You watched what on FlashChat? Me swimming the seawall?" Brent was shocked that his little incident had made it onto Flash-Chat. It was the first time he'd heard about it. "Whose page did you see it on?" he asked Gustavo curiously.

"Dude, I can't even remember. It was trending hard when it first happened. I can't believe you didn't see it," he said, shaking his head. "Hey, that's my ride. What's your name again?"

"Oh, I'm Brent."

"You good, Brent? Do you need a ride somewhere?"

Brent almost said yes until he heard the loud music coming from the car. It didn't look like a good situation. He wasn't trying to get into more trouble.

"Man, I'm straight. I'll see you tomorrow, Gustavo."

"Hey, call me G. Everyone else does. I'll catch up with you later." He jumped into the car with a bunch of kids. One of the boys looked like an older version of Gustavo. Brent was sure they were brothers.

He began his walk to the bus stop. He was proud of himself for not getting into the car, even though it was way more tempting than getting on the uncomfortable bus. He didn't think he could explain his way out of another incident. He was in enough trouble as it was.

The bus took him all around the city. He saw parts of Texsun City he'd never seen. There were long winding roads with water on both sides. There were areas of open land with cattle and horses in the distance. He was definitely in Texas. The scene was like something from an old Western movie.

By the time he made it to the suburbs, he thought he'd been on an adventure. He got off the city bus and took the long walk to his house. He knew his father would be home. He just hoped he could ease in without all the questions about what took him so long.

Brent thought he would be home a lot earlier. He slipped through the front door and up to his room without running into his father. *My plan worked!* he thought. The house was as quiet as a tomb.

He went downstairs, fixed himself a sandwich, got chips, and poured juice. It was only day three of TAC. But it seemed like an eternity since he'd seen Summit. He missed his friends. But he didn't allow himself to think about what was missing. He opened his FlashChat page to see if he could locate his little late-night swim. It was long gone. Nothing stayed on FlashChat. Gustavo got him thinking. *Who had put it online?*

Chapter 6

Too Pushy

He planned to get through the next day without incident. When kids tried to talk to him, he ignored them. He knew he wasn't getting any brownie points by ignoring his classmates. But he wasn't taking any chances.

There was one girl who would not leave him alone. She kept passing him notes in class. She would try to get his attention when nobody was looking. She even sat next to him during lunch. Her name was Shakiera. Everyone called her Baby Shaq. She was a big girl, definitely bigger than him. He wanted no part of it.

During the restroom break, Baby Shaq was determined to get Brent to talk to her. It was like the more he ignored her, the more she sought his attention. Coach Simms always seemed to know what was going on. He caught everything else, but not Baby Shaq hounding Brent.

When he got close to the entrance of the boys' restroom, he felt someone grab him from behind. Before he knew it, he was standing in the girls' restroom. He didn't know how he was going to get out of there without being seen.

"Are you crazy? Why did you do that?" he asked in the meanest whisper he could muster.

"You gonna be my boyfriend," she told him. Oh no, it was Baby Shaq.

"I don't want to be your boyfriend. I mean … it's not you … I don't want to be anybody's boyfriend."

"Well, you ain't got no choice," she warned him, closing in on his personal space. The closer she came to him with her lips pursed, the more distance he tried to put between them. When he couldn't back away any further, he broke for the door. He ran from the restroom as fast as he could, running smack-dab into Coach Simms.

"Mister Bonham, tell me you did not just come out of the girls' restroom."

What could he say? It was true. There was no denying it.

He tried to explain. But Coach Simms was already dragging him to the front office. He could hear laughter from the other students behind him. It was not one of his better moments.

Sitting in the principal's foyer, he couldn't

understand how he kept messing up. He shook his head as he tried to get his story together. How could he explain? He had been strong-armed by a girl!

The principal, Mr. Whitaker, walked out of his office. His face was stern. His jaw looked as though it had been etched into a permanent scowl. Brent thought his dad was tough. This guy looked even worse.

Brent was so nervous. He could feel his legs twitching as he stood to shake the man's hand.

"Mister Bonham, in my office. Now," he said, not wasting words. "I'm surprised by the things I'm hearing. Do you have anything to say for yourself?"

"Sir, I didn't go into the girls' restroom. I was forced in."

The principal removed his glasses from his nose. "And who forced you in?"

"Baby Shaq." He looked down at his legs, embarrassed at having said Shakiera's nickname aloud.

For the first time, the principal seemed to soften. And for a second, he looked as though he wanted to laugh, which upset Brent even more.

"You know I can't be soft on you. I don't want to do this because I know Baby Shaq. I have to give you three days of in-school suspension. There's zero tolerance at TAC. You were caught coming out of the girls' restroom. If there's no punishment, I will be accused of favoritism and all sorts of other things."

"But, Mister Whitaker, I *can't* get in trouble. It wasn't my fault." Brent was pleading with TAC's principal. The principal wasn't moved. He picked up the phone to notify his father of the incident. "Mister Bonham, please."

The principal tried to lessen the blow by explaining that he believed Brent. But a punishment of some sort had to be given. His dad asked to speak to him. He reluctantly took the phone from Mr. Whitaker's hand and put it to his ear.

"I am more than disappointed in you."

"But, Dad, someone pushed me."

"I don't want to hear it, Brent. Save the excuses for your mom. You promised me you would not get in more trouble. Now you are in trouble in the place where you went because you got in trouble!" He hung the phone up before Brent could even respond.

Mr. Whitaker looked as if he felt sorry for him. "I'm sorry, Brent. I really didn't have a choice."

"May I be excused?" he asked his principal dryly.

"Yes, Brent. Your in-school suspension

stay will start tomorrow. You'll serve three days in ISS. Is that clear?"

Brent shrugged his shoulders. He didn't even care anymore. "Yes, sir." There was nothing else he could do to him. He'd heard his father's words loud and clear. *I am more than disappointed in you.* It was the one thing he didn't wanted to do. But now he'd disappointed his father. Again.

Chapter 7

Close Encounter

The next day his father had to accompany Brent to TAC. The ride seemed longer than the one they'd taken on the first day. His father wasn't speaking to him. It was as if Brent was by himself.

They sat down to meet with Mr. Peters, the ISS teacher. He was a short, stocky, and muscular man. Brent hated him on sight.

Mr. Peters spelled out the rules of ISS. He warned Brent that he did not put up with any foolishness in his classroom, especially the type of behavior that Brent had been a part of the previous day.

Brent rolled his eyes. *Where do they find these teachers?* It was as though nobody could understand he wasn't the one at fault. He'd been *pushed*. They were all so quick to judge. Nobody wanted to say Coach Simms was wrong. There was nothing left for Brent to add. His fate was already sealed.

He was escorted to the ISS room when his father left. He copied the rules down and began his assignments. It was as close to jail as a person could get. He was the only person in the room. There was nothing to do except schoolwork, and there was no one to talk to.

At lunch he watched as the other students sat and talked quietly together. He was ushered through the food line and back to ISS. There was no relief. Only a half-day of his three-day sentence had passed. *This is going to be the worst week of my life,* he thought, feeling sorry for himself.

He finished lunch and sat quietly. He could feel his eyelids getting heavy. He knew Mr. Peters would never let him sleep. He could not fall asleep, or he would have more days added to his ISS stay. Of that he was certain. He was fighting off the drowsiness. But every blink made it harder.

Brent closed his eyes just before the ISS door flew open. The door slammed into the whiteboard, sending the dry erase markers flying. He looked to Mr. Peters, who was very angry. Then his eyes went to the door. *Who would be crazy enough to mess up Mister Peters's room?*

It was Jessa McCain. She was furious. "Look, I am *not* staying in here," she informed Mr. Peters. Her voice was loud. Her eyes snapped with anger. "I'm going to call my mom. I need a pass to the front office. This is crazy. They overreact at this school! I am over it. Enough!"

Mr. Peters looked like a man about to lose it. He stepped past Jessa and glanced into the hallway. Then he turned quickly in her direction. He towered over her small frame. Her eyes grew wide as he walked toward her.

"Sit down in that cubicle closest to my desk, or you will regret the moment you stepped foot in this school." He was deadly serious. Brent wasn't sure what Jessa would do next.

She opened her mouth to protest, but no sound escaped her lips. The teacher came closer to her. She retreated to the small cubicle he'd indicated. Mr. Peters bent down over her desk.

"If you make another sound in this room, I will see to it that you never leave ISS. If you don't do as I say, the rest of your seventh grade year will be spent with me at TAC. I don't know who you *think* you are. But you are about to get yourself into some trouble that your daddy can't get you out of."

The teacher was not playing. Brent could tell by his sinister smile. Jessa sat in silence. She looked up at Mr. Peters with sadness.

Brent sat shocked, watching the whole scene unfold. He had never seen Jessa handled like this before. She usually won every argument. She was known for her sharp tongue. Today, Mr. Peters got the best of her. Brent felt sorry for her. He wanted to speak out in her defense. But he was already in enough trouble. He was relieved she'd retreated from the argument.

He wasn't as sleepy anymore. When he got bored, he eyed Jessa curiously. She was a sight for sore eyes. She almost made being in ISS worth it. She was the closest thing to a superstar that he'd ever seen. She was Jessa McCain.

He wished he could talk to her. He wished

they could eat lunch together. Not under Mr. Peters's watchful eye, however. Nobody could do anything with him watching.

The next day, Brent was excited to go to school. ISS was brutal. But being close to Jessa was all he could think about. He was determined to find some opportunity to talk to her, even if it was only for a minute.

They sat quietly not saying a word, just as Mr. Peters wanted it. Then he left to get a cup of coffee. Jessa turned quickly to Brent.

"Hey, are you that kid from the seawall video?"

"Yeah," he answered shyly. He couldn't believe she knew his story.

"That was cra—" she said as Mr. Peters walked back into the room, stopping her midsentence.

For the next two hours, Brent did his work and relived the moment when Jessa talked to him. *What did she mean by that? Was it crazy in a good way? Or was it crazy in a bad way?*

They left for lunch. He searched for an opportunity to ask her and not sound obsessive at the same time. They ate their lunch with Mr. Peters peering down at them, as if they were the scum of the earth.

After lunch, Mr. Peters began to gather his belongings. He informed them that he would be out for the remainder of the day and the next. He left with a warning. If they didn't behave, he would personally see that more days were added to their ISS stay.

A teacher's aide came into the room to relieve him. Mrs. McCabe was a nice lady. As soon as the door closed, she told them that if they finished their work, she would give them some free time.

Brent felt brave. He moved to the cubicle next to Jessa's. He was close enough to talk to her.

Chapter 8

Breathing Room

Hey, what did you mean when you said what I did was crazy? How did you know about the seawall?"

Jessa laughed and flashed her flawless smile. "Are you serious?"

"Yes, of course."

"It was all over FlashChat when it first happened. I can't believe you didn't know."

"Nah," he said, thinking about it. She was

the second person who said they'd watched it on FlashChat. "Who posted it?" he asked her.

"A lot of people. The whole thing was on there up till the police showed up."

"Man," he chuckled, pretending he thought it was cool. He couldn't believe he was notorious. His smile quickly began to fade when he thought about his dad watching the video.

"Wait a minute," Jessa said. "You didn't know they were taping? So the first part when they were setting the whole thing up at Jean's, they really were scamming you?" She started laughing.

Brent started to become uneasy. *They set it up at Jean's?* This conversation was not going as planned. Jessa made it sound as though he had been played. "It wasn't like that. It was my idea. Well, our idea."

"Okay," she said with a sly smile, as if she knew something he did not.

Jessa was starting to make him mad. He opened the novel he was reading for English. He had finished all of his other schoolwork. He didn't feel like talking anymore. She was a foolish girl—pretty and foolish. He could see what people meant.

"Brent," Jessa whispered. "Come on. You're the only person I have to talk to."

"What, Jessa?" He didn't even look up from his book. As far as he was concerned, the conversation was over.

"Do you know why I'm here? It's way worse than why you're here. Way more embarrassing too," she admitted, trying to throw a peace flag.

She had him. He couldn't lie. He'd heard rumors about what Jessa had done to Carson, the new girl at Summit. But Summit kids had ways of exaggerating stories.

Jessa told her tale of betrayal. She told him the truth. Brent had a face she trusted.

She was comfortable with him. She couldn't say that for most of the other kids at TAC.

He listened intently as she told her story. She fell for Holden Smith. They'd been friends since grade school and had grown up doors apart. Everyone in their neighborhood gushed about what a cute couple they'd make one day. She believed it too. Holden seemed to go along with it. He was never really into other girls until he met Carson Roberts.

Brent knew something about the topic since he was in Holden's circle. But his friend was not one to gossip much. And besides, guys didn't talk about girls with each other. It wasn't cool.

"I hated Carson for making him like her. He was supposed to be with me, or so I thought," she lamented. "I don't know anymore. I don't even think Holden is all that now. I'm over it."

Then she told him of her plan to tell all

of Carson's secrets and how it had backfired. Carson's friends had set Jessa up and taped the whole thing. She had no idea what they'd done, so she kept denying it. But Summit's principal showed her the tape. Then her friends threw Jessa under the bus.

"So you see, I'm not trying to pick on you or make fun of you. The same thing happened to me. One video can change your whole life."

He wasn't buying her "I'm a victim too" talk. He knew enough about Jessa's reputation. She was not the nicest person. "What was on my video?" he asked, trying to brace himself.

"Dude, they set you up. It was as simple as that. I'm telling you. At some point, you went to the restroom at Jean's, right?"

"I guess so," he said, trying to remember what happened that night. "Yeah, I definitely did."

"Well, while you were gone, they plotted. They didn't know the police would come and all that. They were trying to get you to swim in the bay. Once y'all made it over the seawall, Coby was going to pretend to be injured. Then you would go alone."

"What if I wouldn't have done it?"

"They said to push you in. It was a dare for them."

"That doesn't make any sense, Jessa."

"What? Why doesn't it?"

"Coby was really bleeding. Plus, I could have been hurt if they pushed me in like that."

"You are so stupid. They don't care about you being hurt. And Coby's bled worse than that before. You just don't want to believe it."

"No, stupid is thinking that you own someone because people put the two of you together since you were little. Then you lash out at anyone who gets too close." Brent gave Jessa a sharp look. "I think people were right about you. You will say or do anything to hurt anybody. You are too pretty to be so mean. And by the way, I know Holden doesn't want you. He never did."

Chapter 9

The Great Escape

Brent stormed out of the ISS room. He could hear Mrs. McCabe calling him to come back. He didn't want to get her in trouble. But he was done. He couldn't look at Jessa's face anymore. He'd wanted to look cool. Instead she'd called him stupid.

He *felt* gullible. He couldn't lie. Why did he think that Coby and his friends wanted to hang out with him? He felt like punching something. He was done with this school. Done with Jessa McCain.

He reached the school's front gate. He had battled with himself for the entire walk. *Am I doing the right thing? Am I just getting into more trouble? What will my father say? I don't even care anymore!* He pushed the gate open.

A hand grabbed his shoulder. It was Coach Simms. He tried to pull free from his grasp, but it only tightened.

"Where do you think you're going, Bonham?" Coach asked him suspiciously.

"I don't know," Brent said, shaking his head. "I just have to get away from here." There was desperation in his voice.

The look in his eyes must have alerted Coach Simms. His voice softened when he responded. "Look, Brent, I know your dad well. This isn't going to play out the way you want it. Can we go talk in my office?"

The answer must have shown on Brent's face. It was last thing he wanted to do. Why would he confide in Coach Simms? That man was the very reason Brent was in ISS in the first place. If he had shown compassion the day Baby Shaq pushed Brent into the restroom, then his world wouldn't be falling apart right now.

"Come on, Brent. Five minutes. What do you have to lose?"

Brent didn't respond. He started walking back toward the school. He pouted all the way there and slumped down in a chair opposite Coach Simms's desk. Coach Simms reached into his mini-fridge and pulled out two sodas. He grabbed two bags of chips. Brent shook his head. This was not a picnic. But Coach put the soda and chips down in front of him.

Even though he was wary, Brent opened the snacks.

"So what was the final straw today?

How did we get to this point? You walked out of ISS and tried to leave campus without permission. That's not acceptable."

Brent shrugged his shoulders. He still had his guard up. He didn't know whom to trust at this point. So many people had betrayed him, including Coach Simms.

"You know they called for the constable to meet you at the gate today, right?" He paused, allowing his words to sink in. "I stopped him. I wanted to have a try before things got serious for you. I can't help you, dude, unless you want to be helped."

Brent took a sip of his soda. He took a deep breath. "That night at the seawall. It was all a setup. They played me, Coach. I thought I was proving I wasn't a clone of my father. That I was my own man. But they didn't care. They wanted to humiliate me, maybe even him. I let them. I let them get away with it."

"How do you know?" Coach asked.

"People keep telling me they saw the video of my humiliation on FlashChat. There're only so many times you hear the same thing before you start to believe it. I never saw it. From what I hear, I *should* be embarrassed. I was looking like a wannabe."

"Well, Brent, you live and you learn. Were you even friends with these guys?"

"No, not really. I was just hanging out."

"When I was a teenager, my own best friend betrayed my trust. He started seeing my girlfriend behind my back. Trust me, it hurts worse when it's somebody you are close to. You never have to see these guys again, unless you want to."

"Nah, I don't have anything to say to that crew. That was a weak move they pulled. I would never do something like that."

"Everybody doesn't have your best interest at heart. I'm not saying to walk around not trusting anybody. But you have to be careful."

"Coach Simms, I never thought we would be here talking like this," Brent said, laughing. "Thank you for looking out for me today."

"Hey, your father has helped so many boys in our community. How could I not help his son? It was the least I could do. Plus, I know Baby Shaq had a lot to do with you being in the girls' restroom the other day. I just couldn't go soft on you, son. I hope you understand."

"Yeah, Coach. I get it."

They had a newfound respect for each other. "Now you can use the desk in here and finish ISS today, unless you want to go back."

"No, Coach. I'm fine where I am."

Chapter 10

A Brighter Tomorrow

Brent thought all night about how he had stormed out of ISS. Hopefully Mrs. McCabe wasn't in trouble. But he was glad it had played out the way it had. He had one goal when he returned to school. He had to apologize to Mrs. McCabe. It was the right thing to do.

Luckily, Mr. Peters was still out. He walked into the quiet ISS room. It was just Mrs. McCabe and Jessa. They both looked up at the same time. Their eyes looked blank, as though he were the last person on earth that they wanted to see.

Brent took his seat. The notebook with his assignments was already on his desk. He opened it up, trying to buy some time. He needed to generate some courage. He'd planned on apologizing. Seeing their faces made him nervous.

It was his last day of ISS, so it couldn't wait any longer. He knew he owed Jessa an apology too. After thinking about what she had told him, he knew she didn't mean him any harm. He had been embarrassed.

Brent kept flipping through his assignment pages: math, English, social studies, science. He wasn't reading, just skimming. He looked up and saw Jessa staring at him. She quickly looked away when his eyes met hers. He knew what he had to do. He stood up and walked over to the desk where Mrs. McCabe was sitting.

"Mrs. McCabe?"

"Uh-huh," she said, not wanting to look at him. He could tell she was angry with him. She wasn't going to let him off easily.

"I just wanted to … um … apologize for yesterday."

"What happened yesterday?" she asked, putting her newspaper down. Her expression said she didn't need an answer. Her body said she wanted one all the same.

She wanted him to recite his bad deeds. She wanted him to spell it out. "I apologize for losing my temper and walking out of the class. I was told something I didn't like. Something I didn't want to hear." He looked over toward Jessa, who was faking a lack of interest in the conversation.

"I'm really, really sorry, Mrs. McCabe.

You don't have to worry about anything like that happening again. At least from me."

She smiled at him and softened. "We all make mistakes, Mister Bonham. Just don't let it happen again. The last thing I wanted to do was call the constable on you. You've always been very respectful."

"Yes, ma'am." Then he whispered, "Do you mind if I talk to Jessa? I promise, no drama."

She looked at him with a face that said it all. He was not getting anywhere, so he used a look that often melted his mother's resolve. He hoped it would change Mrs. McCabe's mind. "Okay," she finally whispered with obvious reluctance. "But no drama. You hear me?"

He sat down next to Jessa McCain. "Jessa?" She turned her back to him. "Jessa, I'm sorry. I didn't mean to blow up like that. I said some pretty mean things. Things I didn't mean. I don't want you to be mad at me, but you have every right. I was hurt. I can't lie. I was a little bit embarrassed too."

"I told you that you didn't have to be. I told you what I'd been through. But you found a way to throw it back in my face. I was only trying to help you."

"I know. I mean … I know that now."

"You were a jerk," she said, sounding wounded.

"Will you forgive me?"

"I guess so. It doesn't help that I'm stuck with you all day. We're cool, Brent Bonham. But that was your only pass."

"That's all I need."

"Now the two of you need to separate and focus on your assignments," Mrs. McCabe announced. "You have a lot to do before the weekend."

Both Jessa and Brent worked dutifully on their assignments. They were done with two periods to spare. Mrs. McCabe was the best. She gave them both free reading time for an hour. And then she let them have free time to talk.

"I expect you both to behave. I want no repeats of yesterday."

In Brent's wildest dreams, he never thought Jessa McCain would want to spend time with him. She was becoming a real person to him—an extremely beautiful real person—but a real person nonetheless. They got comfortable pulling their desks next to each other. They'd learned more about each other in the past two days than they thought possible.

"We go back to regular classes on Monday. I almost like ISS better," Jessa said.

"Girl, you are insane. If Mister Peters were here, you wouldn't be saying that."

"Oh, for sure. I guess we lucked out."

"*I* lucked out. I got to spend time with you." He couldn't believe he said that. Jessa's cheeks turned pink. His were no better. He had never been so bold.

"Brent, you're a mess," she said to him. "Just yesterday you were stomping out of this classroom, so angry with me. And today I'm the best part of ISS." She shook her head.

"I shouldn't have said that, huh? Sorry."

"It's okay. I've enjoyed getting to know you too. You're a pretty cool kid. Not just because you jumped over the seawall."

"I still can't believe I did that. It was so stupid of me. It's not a mistake I'll ever make again. No way."

"You know this little stay at TAC has opened my eyes too, to my own stupidity. You were right yesterday. The things you said about me being dumb when it came to Holden were true."

"Nah, don't listen to me. It's Holden's loss anyway." He couldn't hide things from this girl. He kept giving his feelings away.

Her eyes held his for a minute before she looked away. "Nobody's ever said that to me before. They all say I'm beautiful, Brent. I know that. I look just like my mom. As long as I could remember, I've been more feared than wanted, though. Does that make sense?"

"Maybe to somebody, but not to me. I like hanging out with you. I have a feeling you'll never talk to me again once we get back to Summit."

"That's not true …" she said as her voice trailed off, thinking about when they would talk to or see each other again.

"Yeah, right."

"Can I ask you for a favor?"

"Anything," Brent said.

"Stay away from Coby and his crew. I don't think they mean you any good. They don't even mean good for themselves, much less anybody else."

It was as though she could read his mind. He was going to confront Coby. He wasn't afraid of him like his little minions were. "I don't know if that's a favor I can keep."

"I need you to, please."

The bell rang just in time. They began to gather their belongings. "Have a good weekend, kiddos!" Mrs. McCabe said with a smile.

"You too, Mrs. McCabe," they said in unison. Then the two headed toward the door.

Chapter 11

Let's Have It

It had been a long week. Brent was still being punished. But he had to get out of the house. He didn't think his father would let him. But he had to try. He'd done what was asked of him at TAC. Maybe that would make a difference.

He crept around the house on Saturday, trying not to disturb his father's peace and quiet. He cleaned his room and the kitchen. It wasn't a difficult task. His nanny had pretty much left everything spotless. He needed to look as though he was working hard, so he stayed busy.

Just as he was fluffing the pillows in the living room, his father walked in. "Brent, you're cleaning up?" he asked, surprised.

"Yep. There's really nothing else to do."

"Uh-huh, what do you want?"

"Nothing," Brent said, sounding guilty. "Okay, I'm lying. I want something."

"Spit it out, son."

"I need some type of release. I'm going crazy at TAC. I need to see my friends, Dad. They're all going to the mall today, and—"

"I don't know about that, Brent. It hasn't been long enough yet. You're still getting in trouble at school. I just don't think you're ready for that."

"Dad, I'm at the end of my rope. I really can't take it anymore. I just need a little break. Please," he begged his father.

Mr. Bonham studied his son. He hated being so hard on him. He really did. But he was trying to make him into a man. The world was not going to be kind to him, so he couldn't be either. In that moment, he felt like his own father. He remembered how his father's tough love made *him* feel. It made him waver on his decision with Brent.

He took a deep breath. "I hope you're not going to make me regret this."

"I promise I won't," Brent yelled as he darted from the living room. He took the stairs to his room two at a time. He called his friends to let them know he would meet them at the mall.

He went through his weekend ritual of getting dressed. He edged his short hair—it had been cut only the week before—and got into the shower.

After showering, he added lotion to his body and a little cologne, just as his father had taught him. "You never want to overdo the cologne," his dad would say.

Then he put on a pair of Levi's, a new black long-sleeve T-shirt, some high-tops, and his black puffer vest. He was looking his best. He felt like he was on top of the world.

He went downstairs to let his dad know he was ready.

As soon as he arrived at the mall, he went to Lids to see if there were any new baseball caps that he was interested in buying. Then he sent a text to his friends, letting them know where to meet him. As soon as he walked out of Lids, he saw a group of boys congregating near the arcade. They were loud and rowdy. He could see that one of them was none other than Coby Reynolds.

Immediately, his heart began to race and his blood started to boil. This was the very group that had changed his life. He walked over to Coby, ready to see him squirm. Ready to put him on the spot for what he had done.

He swaggered over, cool as a cucumber. "Coby," he said, interrupting their laugh fest.

"Hey! Look, y'all, it's Lil Bonham. Why you lookin' beefed out, Lil Bonham?"

"Man, I heard about the FlashChat posts. That was so weak, " Brent said.

"My dude, you the one that came out looking weak, not me. How they treatin' you over there at TAC? Tell Coach Simms I say wassup," Coby joked.

Everybody started laughing. They knew they were the ones responsible for Brent's placement there. They had been there enough to know what he was going through. They dapped each other up as they celebrated their victory.

"Man, I know Daddy didn't like his only kid being brought to the very place he took us. Anyway, Lil Bonham, you gonna need to move around. You're welcome to hang out with us next time we go to the seawall."

At that, they erupted in laughter again. Brent was getting even angrier. He got right in Coby's face. They were the same height and about the same size, but Brent wasn't a fighter. Coby, on the other hand, fought for fun. And he always won.

"This not what you want, Lil Bonham. I'm tryin' to tell you. Go home to Daddy."

Brent bumped him in the chest. Coby lunged for him but stopped short of hitting him. In the mayhem, Brent thought he would actually connect and swung his fist with all his might. Coby was fast. He dodged the blow, sending Brent falling to the floor.

D-Boy yelled, "We got another one for FlashChat!" He had recorded everything on his phone.

Brent could hear them laughing as he ran away. He could see his own friends happily coming toward him. He was too upset to stop. He ran past them. He could hear them calling his name. "Brent! What's wrong? Brent!" they yelled. He kept on running. He never turned around.

This was his year of humiliation. He ducked into the movie theater and paid for a ticket for an unpopular film. He climbed the stairs to the top of the theater. He just wanted to be alone. He could have called his father. But there would be too much explaining.

Brent sat in the darkened theater, fuming. He had let Coby's crew mess with him again. He'd given them the power to make him the laughingstock of Texsun City.

Chapter 12

Everybody's Talking

Brent sat quietly stewing in his room for the remainder of the weekend. His father tried to ask him about his night out. But it only made him angry. He didn't want to talk about it. He couldn't confide in his dad. There was nobody to talk to. His friends had been calling. They couldn't understand why he'd run away from them. He was too embarrassed to explain.

He'd never been in a fight before. Not with boys like these. Things had become too aggressive on the football field before, but that was different. It was an organized sport. This was a real fistfight that he initiated. He'd been determined to prove himself. Determined to show that he could hold his own. It didn't work out as planned. Instead of being his own hero, he wound up on the ground without his punch hitting a target.

He took out his iPad and logged on to FlashChat. Nobody sent him the fight he'd gotten into with the most notorious teen in Texsun City. He felt relieved. Maybe Coby's crew wasn't going to be childish enough to post it. He could only hope.

Monday morning his eyes opened and his heart was filled with dread. He didn't want to go to school. He knew his dad wasn't about to let him stay home. But he also needed to get his TAC punishment over with so he could return to Summit. Missing a day wasn't going to allow him to put this whole mess behind him.

When he walked in TAC's gate, he could feel the tension. For a second, he thought he was imagining it. But something was definitely off. Two girls walked past him on the sidewalk. When they saw him, they buried their heads in their jackets, laughing. He thought one of them said, "There he is."

Brent didn't want to be paranoid. But he was starting to feel that way.

Then he entered the cafeteria where everybody met before school. As soon as he walked in, the whole student body erupted in laughter. Ugh. He knew they knew of his humiliation. There was no denying it now. Coach Simms tried to get everyone to quiet down. Brent's presence alone was causing chaos.

Brent turned around and walked out of the cafeteria. He didn't know Coach was on his tail.

"Son! Wait," he yelled, trying to catch up to Brent. "What was that about?" Coach looked confused as he pleaded with Brent to open up to him.

"Nothing, Coach. I knew coming here today was a bad idea. Man, I just need to go."

"Can we go to my office for a second and talk about it? If you still want to leave, I'll be more than happy to help you out. Deal?" He reached out his hand to Brent, who reluctantly shook it.

Brent followed him down a path that went by the cafeteria. He felt like a loser. Like the thugs had won again. He didn't know if he could handle it. This nightmare was turning from bad to worse. He thought about the past few weeks leading up to this moment: One bad decision after another. Putting trust in the wrong people. Trying to fit in where he didn't belong. It all added up to zero.

He walked into Coach Simms's office and wanted to break something, punch something, or scream. The last thing he wanted to do was to sit here and be counseled. Talking would not help. Nobody could help him. *How could someone who doesn't know me help me out?*

Coach Simms could only scratch the surface of Brent's problems. When he walked out of that office door, he knew he would have to face the music alone.

"Are you okay?" he asked Brent sympathetically.

Brent looked away. He couldn't say yes. He didn't feel like saying no. He just shrugged his shoulders.

"Brent, I can only help you if you want to be helped."

Brent looked him squarely in the eyes.

"Did I ask you for help? You asked me to come to your office. Now what? Man, I can't do your little Doctor Phil session today, Coach. I just can't."

He stood abruptly and pushed back his chair. It fell backward and hit the floor. He hadn't meant for it to happen, but his adrenaline was pumping. He couldn't get himself under control. It was too much. The pressure of ridicule had gotten to him. He bolted through the door. He was out of there.

"Brent! Get back here immediately."

He could hear Coach Simms yelling for the constable. He was waiting for Brent at the gate. *This again?* Brent tried to ease past him to the outside world.

"We can do this the easy way or the hard way, Brent. It's all up to you."

"Man, if I stay here today …"

"Man, if you walk out that gate today,"

the constable said, his eyes reflecting the seriousness of Brent's situation.

Brent let go of the gate and walked back up the path. He didn't even bother returning to Coach Simms's office. He went straight to class, took out his spiral notebook, and began his assignments. Putting all his efforts into his schoolwork, he willed himself to go to each of his classes. One by one.

He'd make it through the day. *If* everyone left him alone. Of course, there was always that one kid who couldn't let it go. When the teacher called Brent's name, the kid said, "Lil Bonham is here." It was the same name Coby called him.

All the bad feelings came rushing back. Brent's teacher didn't know what he'd been through. But this smart-mouthed kid sure did.

"Say, dude, I can show you how 'lil' I am better than I can tell you."

"Not if you fight like you did at the mall. Dude, you'd lose a fight with the wind. Oh snap! That's right, you did!"

The whole class laughed. It was definitely not one of Brent's finest moments. He wasn't going to make it out of this class without punching the kid.

He stormed out of the classroom and headed straight to Coach Simms's office, walking in unannounced.

"Brent, you can't keep doing this. This time, I'm calling your father. It's too much."

Brent was breathing hard. His chest looked as if it was going to pop out of his shirt. He held back tears and balled up his fists. His emotions were at a ten. He didn't know if he could calm down. It was all too much for him. Coach Simms couldn't even scare him by saying he was calling his father. Brent just didn't care.

Chapter 13

Daddy Dearest

Brent couldn't lie. His father's presence on campus was enough to rattle him. He felt uneasy listening to Coach Simms as he detailed what transpired over the past week.

His father looked from Brent to Coach Simms in disbelief. He thought Brent had been getting along fine. He looked at his son and saw a different person. The experience at TAC was changing him. He had seen this type of anger before in the boys he worked with. He wanted to help his son. Brent looked like he was shutting down on everybody right before his eyes.

At this point, his father didn't know if he should get stricter or loosen the reigns. Dealing with the boys who came through Living Proof was easy. It was much harder handling his own son. He could see what other parents had been going through with their boys.

Once Coach Simms finished laying all the cards on the table, Mr. Bonham asked if he could have a moment alone with Brent. He could see his son's body tense up. He turned away from his father. Brent was ready to sit there and take it. He knew what was coming.

"Brent, what is happening to you?"

Brent shrugged his shoulders. He wanted to get through this ordeal. What use was there in talking it to death? He couldn't understand the point. Why was his father even here? What was that supposed to accomplish?

"Talk to me, son. Please."

"I don't want to talk, Dad. What's the use of talking about it? That's not going to change anything."

"But you don't have to go through any of this alone. Why were the other kids laughing when you walked into the cafeteria? Did something happen at the mall? You haven't been the same since then."

A tear rolled down Brent's cheek. He cursed himself for not being able to hold it back. *Weak! They were right. They were all right. I'm a loser.*

His father slid his chair closer to his son's. "I was young once too. It's not easy. I know that. I'm here for you, Brent. I know sometimes I seem tough. Right now we have to put it aside. I can't lose you. Look at me … whatever it is, we will get through it. I promise I won't judge you. Just talk to me."

Brent wiped the tears from his eyes and

sat up straight in his chair. He could do this. He needed to tell his father. He began with the mall and how he had tried to stand up for himself. He told him about winding up on the floor and how the kids had videotaped the whole drama.

Then he told him how everyone saw it on FlashChat. All the kids at TAC knew about it. They'd laughed at him. He told it all and held nothing back. It was the hardest thing he had ever done. He was talking to an ex-Marine, someone who could stand up for himself in the face of grave danger.

Brent was more embarrassed in front of his father than in front of his friends. He had let him down, disgraced the Bonham name.

Brent waited as his father digested the whole story. He couldn't look his dad in the eyes. His father reached out and grabbed his son's hand.

"I'm proud of you, Brent. Those boys you confronted are tougher than you even know. When I was your age, I would have never been able to do what you did."

Brent's head whipped toward his father. He wasn't just saying that. Brent could tell he meant it.

"How could you be proud of me when I was humiliated?" he asked.

"Look, everyone falls short of victory every now and then. I wouldn't recommend you going back and confronting them twice. It's like poking a bear. Sometimes, you just have to leave it alone. And plus, it wasn't their fault that you did what you did. Ultimately, it was your decision, right?"

"Yes, sir. It was."

"Well then, you have to find a way to live with that decision. That's what a man does. Don't keep blaming those boys. If you do, then you'll keep falling into the same trap.

You don't have to prove anything to anybody but yourself."

"You're right, Dad."

"Sometimes you learn more when you lose than when you win. Now you need to come up with a plan on how to move forward. Think about it. We'll talk later. Are you going to be okay here today? People are still going to be talking and laughing. And Lord knows what else."

"I think I can handle it," Brent said.

His father stood to get Coach Simms.

"Dad, thanks." Brent stood up and held his hand out to shake his father's hand. Instead of returning the handshake, his dad grabbed him and gave him the tightest hug he had given him in a long time.

"You're a Bonham, son. You have greatness all through you. Don't let anybody make you forget that."

"Yes, sir."

Just then, Coach Simms returned.

"Thank you so much for calling me, Coach," Mr. Bonham said.

"Thank you for coming," Coach Simms responded. "Brent, you good now?"

"Definitely better, Coach. Thanks." He shook his hand. He knew Coach Simms was going out on a limb for him. He knew they had made a few exceptions for him that they didn't make for other students. He knew he was on thin ice. He had no chances left.

Chapter 14

Saying Goodbye

He made it to lunch without anybody picking on him. His whole demeanor changed. It was like he had taken the Kick Me sign off his back. Everyone could tell. He'd gotten his self-respect back. He went through the lunch line and took his tray to his usual table.

Jessa quickly slid into the seat next to him, which was something she had never done before.

"Hey," she said as she pulled her chair closer to his. "Are you okay?"

"I'm fine, Jessa."

"I told you not to confront them. I *told* you," Jessa said.

"Girl, I don't feel like reliving the whole thing. If that's what you've come over here to talk about, then go to another seat. I'm done with that whole thing."

"Look, I just wanted to check on you. This morning I thought you were going to blow a fuse," she said.

"That was this morning. I'm done with it now. Can you be done with it too?"

"Just like that, huh? You're done with it? I don't get you, Bonham." Her eyes were narrowed slits as she analyzed him.

"Well, maybe you're not supposed to, Jessa," Brent said.

She moved back to her normal seat, even though Coach Simms had warned her not to walk around during lunch. Jessa hadn't learned her lesson. She went through life as if the rules didn't apply to her. She went to sit with the girls she'd befriended at TAC, giving Coach Simms a withering look that said, "Now is not the time."

Brent sat in his afternoon classes, his mind full of Jessa McCain. He played back their conversation as he tried to get through his social studies class. When the teacher called on him, he was lost.

Finally it was the last period of the day. He regretted how his conversation with Jessa had ended. He heard her name announced over the intercom to come to the front office. Now his thoughts were clouded. *What are they calling her for? Is she in trouble? Again? Worse, is she leaving TAC?!*

When the bell rang to dismiss students for the day, she stood outside his classroom.

He walked straight to her, like he knew why she was there.

"I got my release papers," she said, holding them tightly in her hand. Her eyes sparkled. She was practically floating.

Students were talking and moving all around them. But Brent couldn't hear or see anything except Jessa. If he *thought* he regretted their conversation before, he *knew* it now. He hadn't treated her right.

"I'm sorry about earlier." He didn't know what else to say.

"It's okay. I shouldn't have tried to force you into talking about it. It was none of my business. I was just trying—"

"To be a good friend. You were the best friend I've had here," he admitted. "Now you're leaving."

"You weren't so bad yourself, Bonham. You were the best part about coming to TAC."

He started to blush. He never would have imagined something like this happening to him here. That Jessa McCain would say these words to him.

"Hey, don't feel pressured to hang out with me when you get back to Summit. I know you have your own crew. The whole cheer-leading squad is waiting for you. We live in two different worlds there, so you don't have to feel bad. I know that we'll probably never talk again."

By this time, the entire school had emptied out. They were alone. Jessa looked at Brent and whispered to him, "You don't have to worry about that."

Then she leaned forward and kissed him on the lips. Brent thought he would pass out. He didn't know how she managed to drain the life out of him with one kiss.

"Hey, the bus is going to leave. Let's get out of here," she said.

He felt like he couldn't move, but he did. One foot in front of the other. This was a day he would never forget. He had the silliest, goofiest look on his face as he boarded the bus. His first kiss was with Jessa McCain. Jessa McCain!

TAC had turned out to be the best experience of his life. For that kiss—from that girl—it was *so* worth it.

By the time he got home from school, he was on cloud nine. His dad was happy to see that he'd made it through the day with a new lease on life. His Brent was back.

His dad was positive their talk had made a huge impact. Brent was sure their talk and that oh-so-memorable kiss had flipped his world upside down. Everything that was so bad now felt so good.

"You want to grab a bite to eat at Saltgrass?" his father asked him.

"You bet!" Brent yelled, grabbing his jacket. "Saltgrass during the week, Dad?"

"Really? I offer to take you to your favorite restaurant and you question me?" his dad asked, laughing.

"Not at all. Forget I mentioned it."

Chapter 15

Dinner for Three

They arrived at Saltgrass. It was packed as usual. His father had already made reservations and requested their favorite booth.

Brent thought it felt strange coming here without his mom. They hadn't been here since she left for D.C. He almost felt guilty for enjoying the outing without her.

They ordered their drinks and munched on homemade bread smeared with butter until the server returned. Brent toyed with his phone as his father answered a few emails.

"Dad, today really turned me around," he said to his father. "I can't thank you enough for what you did for me, coming up to the school and all."

"I did what I was supposed to do. You are my son. I'll always be there for you."

His words made Brent smile. He had been so angry with his dad. He was just happy that they were able to get past that bump in the road.

Just when he was feeling on top of the world, someone walked up to their table. His back was turned, but Brent sensed it was a woman. He looked at his father, whose face lit up. Brent felt himself getting uneasy. He wanted his father to himself. This was their family time. He turned and looked. He wanted to see who was intruding on their night out.

"Mom?" he said, shocked. "But … what are you doing here?"

"Boy, get up and give your mother a hug. I came home to see my baby."

He wanted to cry. But he couldn't cry in the restaurant, not with everyone looking. He jumped up and hugged her. She rubbed his hair gently and kissed him on his cheek, then his forehead. She held him away from her. "Did you get taller, or just more handsome since I left?"

"Probably both," Brent said with a smile. He turned back to his father, who watched both of them with joy. "You knew all along. You tricked me," Brent exclaimed.

"Let my wife sit down, please," Mr. Bonham said, winking in her direction.

She bent down and kissed her husband. Then he stood up and hugged her until she forced him to let go. Their eyes met before she slid into the booth next to Brent.

"Mom, are you home for good?" Brent asked her.

"I'm home for now. It'll be a while before I have to go back to D.C., so you are stuck with me."

"That's the best news I've heard all day. I can't believe you two kept this from me."

"We really didn't know, Brent. It just so happens we acquired the signatures we needed to put the bill into motion. It was a lot of hard work. As soon as I knew I could come home, I was on the next plane to Texas. I *missed* you." She reached out for Brent's hand, pulling him close to her in the booth.

It was what he'd been missing all along. He snuggled with his mom, not caring what anybody thought. "I missed you too," he told her. Then he looked at his dad. "But I think the father-son alone time was good. Dad and I needed that. But it sure is good to have you home, Mom."

"I can't argue with that," his father agreed. He looked proudly at his family.

They dined together, united, and went home that night as a family. Just when Brent turned out his bedroom light, his mother came in and sat on the edge of his bed.

"I hear you've been having a rough time without Mama," she said.

"It's true." He was embarrassed at how he'd acted. It was one thing to let his father down. But his mother? That was even worse.

"Are you okay now? Is there anything you want to talk about?" She rubbed his head, smoothing his hair down.

"Mom, I think I have it all under control now. I really do."

"That's a good thing, Brent. If you need me, you know where to find me."

"Yes, ma'am. Just don't leave again. I don't like it when you're not here. It's just … harder," he confessed.

"Baby, Mama can't be with you all the time. You're learning. I love the man you are becoming. You are going to make mistakes. Just learn from them and everything will be fine. Okay? Good night." She gently kissed him on the cheek and left.

The smile on Brent's face probably could have been seen by satellite. He was beyond happy. His heart was singing. This had been a day to remember. First the mending of his relationship with his father. Then a kiss from the most beautiful girl at TAC and Summit Middle School. And finally the return of his mother. No day would ever compare.

He finally dozed off after replaying the memories so many times he couldn't keep count. He had to go back to TAC tomorrow. But everything felt different. Everything *was* different. Most of all, he was different. That was the most important part of all.

Want to Keep Reading?

Turn the page for a sneak peek at Shannon Freeman's next book in the Summit Middle School series: *All About My Selfie*.

ISBN: 978-1-68021-009-5

Chapter 1

The Swansons

*E*mma Swanson was always trying to find her place in Texsun City. It wasn't her fault that she'd been shunned by her peers. She wasn't sure who to blame. She just knew she didn't measure up somehow.

Her family had money and beachfront property. Emma had every luxury a girl could want. But it wasn't enough. She'd tried out for cheerleading twice. She didn't make the cut either time. Then she gave up trying to be popular. She was over trying to fit in.

Instead, she tried to find things that interested her. Like art or horseback riding. She wasn't seeking anyone's approval. It didn't matter.

She heard the rumors about her grandfather's fortune. How other families had not been as successful. It was easy to blame him. Nobody complained when the rice industry was booming. Money grew on trees. Then taxes took their toll. Some found it hard to stay afloat. But not Emma's grandfather.

Thomas Swanson had been a smart man. He was able to spread his money around. In other words, he hid it. Then he bought out his partners. He passed his fortune down to his children.

Many resented his quick thinking. Some moved on to different businesses. Others just went under. Emma didn't know how much of the story was true. She believed some of it had to be. She loved her grandfather. He was shrewd. He knew how to handle money. One thing was for sure, he loved his family. That was what mattered to Emma.

Unfortunately, his dealings with his former rivals made Texsun City a difficult place to live for Emma. And made Summit Middle School especially tough. Emma could ask him to donate money to build a better library. Or ask him to make some grand gesture that would create goodwill. Grease the path for her. But she didn't want to.

Emma wanted to be accepted for who she was. If the other girls wanted to hate her because of family rivalry, then so be it. She knew one day she would figure it out on her own.

When Carson Roberts showed up at Summit Middle School, Emma found "her tribe." The girls instantly hit it off. Who knew opening Summit to so many new faces would be Emma's salvation? It was just what she needed. And at the perfect time.

Carson was a breath of fresh air. They had a common enemy. And they found a kindred spirit in Mai Pham. Emma had known Mai for many years. But they had never really opened up to each other. Each was dealing with her own walls, built to protect them from the SMS mean-girl cliques.

"Emma! Come downstairs, darling," Miss Arina called.

Miss Arina was Emma's rock. She had been her nanny since infancy. She was the constant in her world. Her nanny got Emma through the hard times. Her parents had a lot on their plate. Her father ran Swanson Rice. Her mother worked tirelessly with Texsun City nonprofits.

Emma ran down the staircase to her nanny. Miss Arina's solid frame was waiting in the foyer, wearing a starched white apron over her clothes.

"Your father just arrived in town," she said in her heavy Russian accent. "Your parents are taking you out for dinner tonight. You need to get ready."

"Mommy and Daddy?"

"Yes, dear. Now go get pretty, please. Put on something that makes those green eyes pop."

Miss Arina hugged Emma tightly. Then she retreated into the kitchen.

Emma returned to her room. She looked through her closet, debating what to wear. She already knew where they were going to eat. Whenever her parents called for dinner out, they sat down at Sartain's.

Where else did people from Texsun City go when they all got together? Sartain's wasn't fancy, but it was good. They had the best barbequed crabs in the area. You could eat as much as your stomach could handle. Plus, Sartain's was mellow. They would be able to talk. Catch up on their lives.

Emma decided to go casual. She slipped on her green cashmere sweater, skinny jeans, and brown Uggs. She was ready for some barbequed crabs.

When the limousine arrived in the circular driveway, Miss Arina called for her. Emma ran to meet her parents, who were waiting patiently for their only child. Her father hugged her tightly. Her mother watched her with loving eyes.

"How's my girl?" she asked when Emma was allowed to come up for air.

"I'm fine, Mom. Are you here for a while this time?"

"I am, darling. Thank God."

They talked until they pulled up at Sartain's. They were seated immediately.

Then they ordered. The family continued catching up while they ate. Their fingers tingled from all of the wonderful, finger-licking spices.

"It's good to be back in Texas," her father announced.

"Yes it is," Mrs. Swanson agreed. "So how is Mai doing with her singing?" she asked Emma.

"She's fine. We have a few shows coming up soon. And I wanted to ask a favor of you both."

"Anything, dear," her father replied.

"Well, I wanted to see if it would be okay for Mai to perform at the Rice Festival this year."

"That's an excellent idea," her mother said approvingly.

"We have some big names coming into town for that," her father said. "But I'm sure we can add her to the roster. We'll find a place."

"Oh, thanks, Dad. She is going to be thrilled. I can't wait to tell her."

They continued eating until they couldn't possibly eat another crab. They sat stuffed in their chairs, vowing that they needed a month to recover before they could return to their favorite family restaurant.

About the Author

Shannon Freeman

Born and raised in Port Arthur, Texas, Shannon Freeman is an English teacher in her hometown. As a full-time teacher, Freeman stays close to topics that are relevant to today's teenagers.

Entertaining others has always been a strong desire for the author. Living in

California for nearly a decade, Freeman enjoyed working in the entertainment industry, appearing on shows like *Worst-Case Scenario*, *The Oprah Winfrey Show*, and numerous others. She also worked in radio and traveled extensively as a product specialist for the Auto Show of North America. These life experiences, plus the friendships she made along the way, have inspired her to create realistic characters that jump off the page.

Today she enjoys a life filled with family. She and her husband, Derrick, have four beautiful children: Kaymon, Kingston, Addyson, and Brance. Their days are full of family-packed events. They also regularly volunteer in their community.

Freeman's debut series, *Port City High*, is geared to high-school readers. When asked to write for middle school students, she knew it would be a challenge, but one that she was up for. *Summit Middle School* is the author's second series. She hopes these stories will reach students from many different backgrounds. "It is definitely a series where middle-grade students can read about realistic life experiences involving characters just like them. Middle school can be a challenge, and if I can help students navigate through that world, then I have met my goal."

Freeman loves writing a series that her children and numerous nephews and nieces can enjoy.